This book belongs to

_____

For Jerry and Lynn Rudy,
my favorite parents

Henry Holt and Company, *Publishers since 1866*
Henry Holt® is a registered trademark of Macmillan Publishing Group, LLC
120 Broadway, New York, NY 10271 • mackids.com

Library of Congress Control Number: 2019941045
ISBN 978-1-250-18604-1

Our books may be purchased in bulk for promotional, educational, or business use.
Please contact your local bookseller or the Macmillan Corporate and Premium Sales Department
at (800) 221-7945 ext. 5442 or by email at MacmillanSpecialMarkets@macmillan.com.

First edition, 2020 / Designed by April Ward
The illustrations in this book were built, photographed, and edited by the author.
Characters and sets were constructed of wool felt and found materials.
Lighting by Sally Foster of Far and Away Productions.

Printed in China by Toppan Leefung Printing Ltd., Dongguan City, Guangdong Province

1 3 5 7 9 10 8 6 4 2

SOOTYPAWS

A Cinderella Story

MAGGIE RUDY

Henry Holt and Company

New York

There once was a mouse, and her life was no fun.

When she was a baby, her mother was eaten by a tabby cat, and her father took a new rat wife with two daughters. Then he died, too, leaving her alone with her stepmother and stepsisters.

The steprats had no love for the little mouse,
and they made her do all the work while they
sat on cushions eating coconut bonbons and
reading magazines.

At night she curled up in the fireplace ashes to keep warm, and so they called her Sootypaws.

Sootypaws missed her parents and wished most of all that someone would love her. She thought about running away, but where could a little mouse go, all alone?

The only friends Sootypaws had were the wild creatures who lived in the garden. She brought crumbs from the table for the ants and gathered the fur from her comb for the bluebird to line its nest.

She complimented the frog on his tadpoles, and she always gave the rosebush a drink of water.

"Daughters!" cried the stepmother one morning. "There is a ball tonight at the palace! The King wishes to find a wife for his son, the Prince!"

"Ball! Palace! Prince!" shrieked the sisters.

"Yes, and why shouldn't he choose one of you?" said their mother. "I'm sure you are as lovely as any in the kingdom."

A muffled snort came from the fireplace.

"Oh, there you are, Sootypaws," said the stepmother. "Prepare our gowns *at once*!"

All day long, Sootypaws washed and ironed while the rats gossiped about the ball. She tried to imagine the music, the banquet, the whirling dancers.

Oh, how I wish I could see them! she thought.

When the steprats, powdered and frilled, left for the ball that evening, Sootypaws went outside to sit by the moonlit pond.

The frog rose to the surface and
looked at the droopy mouse.
"Anything wrong?" he asked.
"Oh," Sootypaws said wistfully,
"I just wish *I* could go to the ball, too."

"You *will* go to the ball, then," replied the frog, "for there is a full moon and it is a very good night for wishes."

"How can I go to the palace?" Sootypaws asked. "They will turn me away in these raggedy clothes."

The moon quivered, and a single rose petal floated down.

"Your gown," whispered
the rosebush as a flurry
of petals softly wrapped
around Sootypaws.

"I will give you my best feathers for a fan," said the bluebird.

"You have never knocked down my webs," said the spider, "so I will weave my finest lace for your collar."

"Take these," chanted the ants, "and thanks for the crumbs!" They held up a pair of exquisite green slippers with heels made of rose thorns.

Everybody joined together to help Sootypaws, who had been so kind to them.

The apple tree dropped its reddest fruit for a coach, and four fireflies lit the lamps.

"We will pull you!" said two blue-bellied lizards, and they showed off their muscles with some push-ups.

A great moth unfurled its velvet wings into a cloak, and a coachman in splendid green livery handed Sootypaws into the carriage.

"Thank you, dear friends, thank you!" cried Sootypaws as she rolled away. "I'll never forget this magical night!"

"Goodbye!" they called. "Have a wonderful time!"

"But be back by midnight," warned the bluebird, "for that is when the moon magic wears off."

What dazzling sights Sootypaws saw at the palace!

Chattering voices rose above the music, and the ballroom sparkled with a thousand jewels.

Everybody turned to look at the beautiful stranger, and a murmur ran around the room.

"Who is that?" they whispered. "Who is she?"

"May I have this dance?" asked a mouse with diamond buckles on his shoes.

"Oh yes!" said Sootypaws,
and they spun onto
the floor.

All evening, Sootypaws and the Prince (for that was who he was) danced and laughed and ate strawberry cream puffs. Even though her feet hurt, Sootypaws was having such an exciting time that she forgot the bluebird's warning.

When the clock struck midnight, she snatched her
paw away from the Prince and scurried outside.
"Wait!" he cried. "I don't know your name!"

Poor Sootypaws! Her coach was just a red apple lying on the ground. All that remained were the shoes with the rose-thorn heels.

"Drat these pointy things!" said Sootypaws, and she kicked them off and ran barefoot into the night.

When the Prince ran
after her, all he found were
the little green slippers
lying on the path.

"Desperately Seeking Damsel," read the stepmother the next morning. "The Prince will marry the lady whose foot fits the slipper."

"He is looking for that mysterious mouse," said one of the sisters sourly. "He didn't take his eyes off her all night."

"I'm *sure* I could wear that slipper," declared the second sister. "I have such teeny-tiny feet."

"Mine are even smaller," said the first sister. "The Prince will surely marry *me*."

When the Prince arrived that
afternoon with the green slippers,
the rat sisters pulled and squeezed
and curled their toes, but they could
not force their feet into the tiny shoes.
  "Let me try," said a voice.
  The Prince spun around.

"It's you!" he cried.

"Yes, Prince," said Sootypaws. "I am so glad to see you."

"I've found you," the Prince said, "but I don't know your name."

"The rats call me Sootypaws," she replied, "but my mother named me Rosie. Do I have to put those thorny shoes back on?"

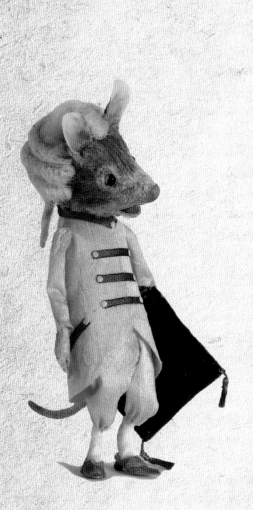

"Of course not," said the Prince, "but will you marry me, Rosie?"

"I love you, Prince," said Rosie, "but I don't want to get married or be a princess in a palace. I want to run free and have adventures!"

"So do I," said the Prince, standing up. He scowled down at his fancy shoes.

"Look at these dumb things," he said. "What are they even for?"

Rosie took his paw.

"Leave them behind," she said. "We can go together."

So the Prince kicked off his silly shoes and ran away with Rosie.

They lived a life full of adventures, and they never wore shoes again.

And, of course,
they lived mousily
ever after.